BOB WADE
95

Dear Wendy & Barbara -
We can't wait to welcome you both
to the land of Big Hair, Oil Wells and
Armadillos (and Neimans).   Much love
                                Bob & Mark

COWGIRLS

BY BOB WADE
FOREWORD BY LINDA GRAY

SALT LAKE CITY

Cowgirls is dedicated to people everywhere who continue to embrace the cowgirl spirit. I am indebted to those who assisted in bringing my cowgirl artwork and this book to life: Gibbs Smith, publisher, and Caroll Shreeve, editor; Thomas E. Berry, art director: Kinara Graphics; and Linda Gray, Lisa Wade, Fern Sawyer Family, David Hale Smith, Western States Arts Federation, Bell Photo, James Hart Photography, anonymous rodeo photographers, Art Wear, Tangibles, Leanin' Tree, collectors, and gallery representatives.

I thank you.   —Bob Wade

First edition
97 96 95   3 2 1

Text and photographs copyright © 1995 by Bob Wade

This is a Peregrine Smith Book, published by
Gibbs Smith, Publisher
P.O. Box 667
Layton, UT 84041

Design by Thomas E. Berry, Kinara Graphics
Printed and bound in Hong Kong

ISBN 0-87905-685-1

"The Goddesses of the Wild West" . . . that's what I call the piece I bought from Bob Wade in 1985, when I first saw the "Cowgirls." I knew they had to come home with me. The painting now hangs in a very special place in my home. As I pass by it each day, I am struck by its miraculous blend of masculine and feminine, strength and serenity.

Bob Wade understands the power of period pieces. He selected a magical black- and-white vintage photograph, and brought these "Goddesses" to life in a subtle yet compelling way with his skillful hand tinting.

Bob has captured the true pioneer spirit of these women of the West — fearless and feminine. They are feisty women, taking on a man's world, breaking taboos, living on the road, marrying and divorcing, competing with the best. When looking at them, vivid images come to mind — images of a cattle baroness, a madame, a suffragette, a sharpshooter, a doctor, an outlaw, a teacher. Whether she be riding a bronco, wrestling a steer, or the first business woman who ran a dress shop or a saloon, Bob honors the passion, the pride, and the power of these "Goddesses of the West" with his art.

The "Cowgirls" are a lively combination of strong, powerful, capable, and gutsy women with dignity as big as their style. I've given them names. Names like Lilyan, Harriet, Helen, Lila . . .

I will be forever grateful to Bob for providing an art piece that inspires my soul, makes me smile, makes me wonder what it was like to be a woman at that time. He gave me a gift of a few women "friends" with great attitudes and outrageous outfits. I appreciate and love Bob Wade for bringing his art to us all. Isn't that where it should be?

—Linda Gray

Bob Wade with cowgirl
friend, Fern Sawyer

Native Texan Bob Wade lived all over Texas as a young "Buckaroo" playing on the set of the movie "Giant" and watching his second cousin Roy Rogers appear at rodeos. Wade's "Photo Works" are the result of 25 years of experimentation with large-scale photography and color enhancement of black- and-white vintage photos. By transferring images to photo linen and airbrushing transparent acrylic over the enlargement, the artist "integrates" photography with painting. Some mural-size paintings are as long as 30 feet. A masters degree in painting and three fellowships from the NEA led to his national and international exhibitions, including Biennials at the Whitney Museum in New York and The Museum of Modern Art in Paris, France. His work is in numerous corporate and museum collections including Chase Manhattan Bank, A T & T, and the Menil Collection, Houston.

EARLY RANGE RIDERS

Long before the term *cowgirl* came into popularity, ranch women rode the range for business and pleasure, wearing split skirts. Many ranch women became rodeo performers and thus Cow Girls.

LUCILLE AND WHITE HORSE

Lucille Mulhall was one of the earliest professional performers, appearing at age ten in the 1905 Madison Square Garden show in New York. Becoming the Lady Champion Roper of the World, and the Queen of the Range, Lucille was the first woman rodeo producer in history. Will Rogers promoted her as the "original cowgirl."

TEXANA

Texana was the typical sharpshooter who performed in
Wild West shows and on the rodeo circuits. While not the
horsewoman of the arena, nevertheless this crack shot in calf- and
snake-skin skirt exudes the cowgirl spirit.

THIRTEEN COWGIRLS

Cowgirls performed around the U.S. as well as in Europe and the Orient.
By 1926 places like London, New York, and Chicago eagerly awaited
razzle-dazzle action by the likes of Lulu Belle, Tillie, Dixie, Fannie, Goldie, Flaxie,
Thena Mae, Fern, Tad, Fox, Prairie Rose, Lorena, Texas, Reine, Bea, Ruby, Velda,
Montana Belle, Jewel, and Brida.

RODEO WOMEN

Carrying quirts and as many hats as it took, this trio included M
(center) and Ruby Dickey (right). Starting as a young East Coast
Mildred trained in the circus and the 101 Wild West Sh
before excelling in trick, bronc, and steer riding.

PRAIRIE ROSE

In addition to her top-notch athletic accomplishments, Prairie Rose
became a flamboyant standout in her handmade outfits that were
custom-fitted with fur, ostrich feathers, silk, and sequins.
Both fans and judges were impressed.

RUTH AND SPOTTY

Ruth Roach learned to ride while growing up on farms in Missouri.
Wearing bloomers, bows, and boots with hearts, Ruth performed in Europe i
1914 and 1924. A champion lady bronc rider through the 1930s, the blond
"Golden Girl of the West" also did publicity stunts by riding through
hotel lobbies and in parade ceremonies.

TWINS
Cowgirls performing in Mexico returned with tricks of the trade and costume ideas from bullrings and rodeos. They adopted bolero jackets and custom boots elaborately embellished with stitched designs.

KITTY'S COWGIRLS
And the winners are: (left to right) Bea Kirnan, Prairie Rose, Mabel Strickland, Princess Mohawk, Ruth Roach, Kitty Canutt, and Prairie Lillie. Kitty Canutt had a diamond in her front tooth that she pawned on occasion.

COWGIRL AND THE LETTER
Over one hundred women followed the harsh rodeo circuit
by 1916. That year, Catherine Wilkes became World Champion
Bronco Buster in Miles City, Montana.

TRICK RIDER UNDER HORSE
Balance, coordination, physical fitness, and nerve were all prerequisites for "going under the belly." Jockey caps and rubber-soled shoes made routines easier for these athletes. Eleanor Heacock, Faye Blesing, Bonnie Gray, and Reine Hafley were among the daring greats.

WOOLY GIRLS

While angora chaps were occasionally worn by performing cowg...
warmth and for show, these woolies were props used by photo studi...
souvenirs for "wannabe" cowgirls in hats, holsters, and high h...

MARGE RIDIN' IT OUT

ge and Alice Greenough were among the approximately twenty
riding broncs in the early days. Known as "The Wild Bunch," these
ere bucked off, stepped on, rolled on, and dragged through the dirt
by their luck of the draw. Many were hurt—some died.

HIGH IN THE SADDLE
Evolving from early Russian circus trick riders, rodeo performers thrilled crowds with "stands," "vaults," and "drags." Wearing colorful silk and satin blouses, bloomers, sashes, and scarves, these daredevil cowgirls were truly fabulous.

DOROTHY SMILING

When Dorothy Morrell rode bucking broncs, she rode with style and beauty.
These attributes also took her to Hollywood, where the studios took classic
movie-star photos. From stunts to stand-ins to leading ladies, *real* cowgirls
were needed in the film industry.

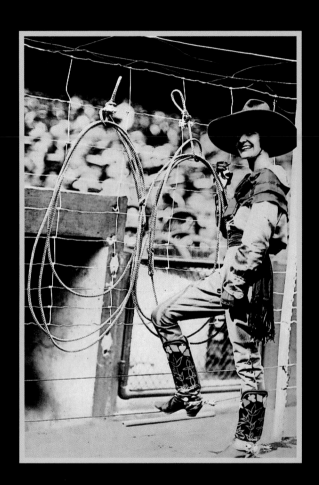

MABEL WITH TWO ROPES
Mabel Strickland wore boots custom-made by her father as she competed
in relay races and trick riding in Walla Walla, Washington. Mabel became the
first Rodeo Queen of the Pendleton Roundup and worked with
Bing Crosby in *Rhythm on the Range* in 1937.

COWGIRLS GET THE BLUES
Sometimes cowgirls *did* get the blues. They got divorced, went broke, felt lonely, cracked their ribs, and got beat out by the competition. But their faces show they never got down and out.

COWGIRLS ON A FENCE
As world travelers, rodeo women brought home fashion
ideas from New York, Europe, and Hollywood. Obviously it was
time to experiment with hairstyles—extra curvy, curly, and wavy.

MABEL TYING A STEER
Mabel Strickland gave up farming to become the Lovely Lady of Rodeo, the Crown Princess of Rodeo, and Cheyenne's All-Around Cowgirl. Roping and tying steers was a favorite event of hers, and her finesse was also appreciated in Hollywood.

COWGIRLS OF THE HOOD
Many cowgirls worked with movie studios doing stunts and action
promotions. Rodeo and Wild West show themes, acted out by Tom Mix,
hy Morrell, and Hoot Gibson, became crowd pleasers. Wild West shows
were eventually replaced by western action on the silver screen.

COWGIRLS AND HARLEYS
The show must go on, so daring cowgirls rode the range on horses,
Harleys, trains, and planes. Proficient at hog tyin' and fearless at hog ridin',
you just can't keep a good cowgirl down.

FERN ON THE FENCE

New Mexico's Fern Sawyer roped bulls and trained horses, but truly loved beating men in cutting- horse competition in the 1930s and 1940s. Known for her chic outfits and boot collection, Fern rode hard, drank hard, and cussed often as both contestant and arena judge. The National All-Around Cowgirl Champion and cofounder of the National Cutting Horse Association died in 1993–with her boots on.